For all my teammates on *Foul Play* —S.K.

For Jackson and Parker Lily —J.M.

Text copyright © 2011 by Stephen Krensky
Illustrations copyright © 2011 by Joe Morse

Millbrook Press
A division of Lerner Publishing Group, Inc.
241 First Avenue North
Minneapolis, MN 55401 USA

For reading levels and more information,
look up this title at www.lernerbooks.com.

The images in this book are used with the permission of: © Hulton Archive/Getty Images, p. 30 (top/left); AP Photo, p. 30 (bottom/left); © Bettmann/CORBIS, p. 30 (right).

Library of Congress Cataloging-in-Publication Data

Krensky, Stephen.
  Play ball, Jackie! / by Stephen Krensky ; illustrated by Joe Morse.
    p.   cm.
  Summary: On April 15, 1947, Matt Romano and his father watch the Brooklyn Dodgers season-opener, during which Jackie Robinson, a twenty-eight-year-old rookie, breaks the "color line" that had kept black men out of Major League baseball. Includes facts about Jackie Robinson's life and career.
    ISBN: 978–0–8225–9030–9 (lib. bdg. : alk. paper) — ISBN: 978–0–7613–7261–5 (EB pdf)
    1. Robinson, Jackie, 1919–1972—Juvenile fiction. [1. Robinson, Jackie, 1919–1972—Fiction. 2. Baseball—Fiction. 3. Race relations—Fiction. 4. Brooklyn Dodgers (Baseball team)—Fiction.] I. Morse, Joe, 1960– ill. II. Title.
PZ7.K883Pl 2011
[E]—dc22   2010027270

Manufactured in the United States of America
2 – CG – 7/1/15

PLAY BALL, Jackie!

Stephen Krensky

illustrations by Joe Morse

M Millbrook Press/Minneapolis

"PLAY BALL!" called the home plate
umpire at Ebbets Field.
It was Major League Baseball's Opening
Day—April 15, 1947. The Brooklyn Dodgers
were playing the Boston Braves.

More than 25,000 fans settled into their seats. One of them was Matty Romano. He was sitting in the grandstand behind third base. The spring afternoon was cool, and the air smelled of peanuts and popcorn.

Matty was a big Dodgers fan. The team had finished second in the National League in 1946. Matty knew they would do better this year. Just a few more wins, and they could make it to the World Series.

A lot of kids were in the stands, even on a school day. Matty's father, like many others, had taken him out early for the afternoon game.

"Free tickets," his father had told him. "One of the guys at work refused to go."

"Really?" said Matty. "Someone gave up tickets on Opening Day? He must be crazy."

Matty's father shook his head. "Not crazy," he said. "Disgusted."

"About what?" Matty asked.

His father pointed at first base.

The first baseman
was pounding his fist
into his mitt. Matty
knew his name—Jackie
Robinson. He was a
black man. For a lot
of people, that was a
problem.

NEGRO *Stars* LEAGUE
BASEBALL

Up till now, black men didn't play Major League Baseball. Oh sure, they played baseball all the time. And some of them were really good, like Satchel Paige and Josh Gibson. But they played only in the Negro Leagues, where everyone was black.

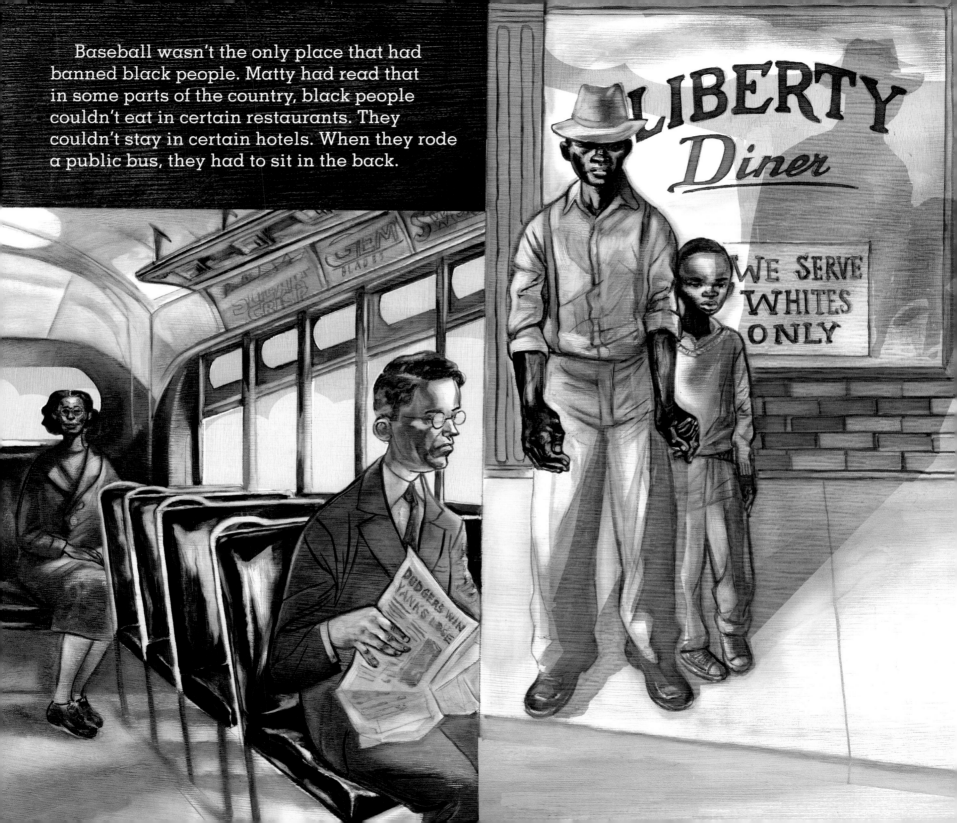

Baseball wasn't the only place that had banned black people. Matty had read that in some parts of the country, black people couldn't eat in certain restaurants. They couldn't stay in certain hotels. When they rode a public bus, they had to sit in the back.

EXTRA!

THE WEATHER

THE DAILY NEWS

TODAY'S NEWS

WAR - IT'S ALL OVER

Times seemed to be changing, though. Black soldiers had fought for the United States in World War II. Now that the war was over, black people were doing some things they couldn't do before. One of those things was to take part in Major League Baseball games.

Tuskegee 33rd Airmen Fighting Group

"What do you think, Dad?" Matty asked. "Should Jackie Robinson be here?"

"I want to see the best players out there," said his father. "I don't care what color they are. Remember, your grandfather came to America from Italy. Lots of people didn't give him a chance, either. He looked strange to them. His clothes were shabby, and he spoke English with an accent. He had to work long and hard for everything he got."

Italia

NEW YORK

UNIONE B

La Liber

DOMEN

PREZZ

Matty remembered hearing his grandfather's stories around the kitchen table. Everyone deserved a chance for a better life—his grandfather and Jackie Robinson too.

Matty watched the Braves' shortstop,
Dick Culler, come to the plate. Dodgers'
pitcher Joe Hatten was on the mound.
"COME ON, HATTEN!" Matty's
father yelled at the pitcher.
"SHOW HIM THE HEAT!"

Hatten pitched.
One out. Two outs.
Three outs.
  "Three up, three
down," said Matty.
"Just the way I like it."

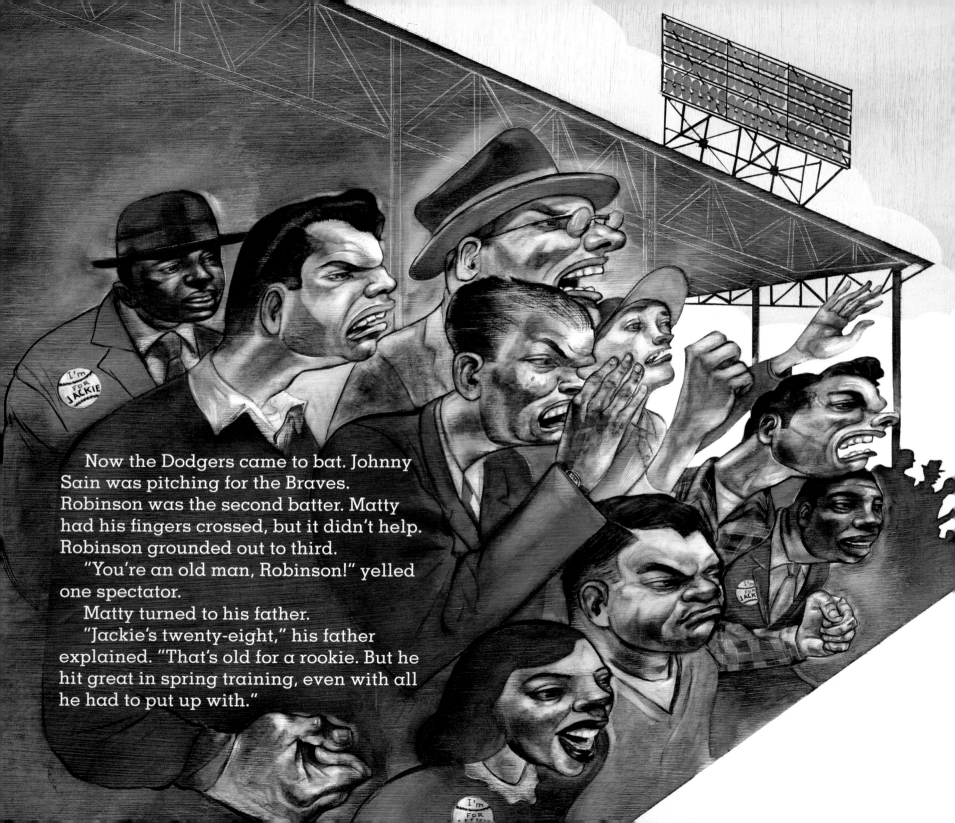

Now the Dodgers came to bat. Johnny Sain was pitching for the Braves. Robinson was the second batter. Matty had his fingers crossed, but it didn't help. Robinson grounded out to third.

"You're an old man, Robinson!" yelled one spectator.

Matty turned to his father.

"Jackie's twenty-eight," his father explained. "That's old for a rookie. But he hit great in spring training, even with all he had to put up with."

"Like what?" asked Matty.

"I read about it in the paper," said his father. "Some players on other teams gave him a hard time. And he couldn't stay at the same nice hotels as the white ballplayers."

Matty shook his head. He noticed that some people in the crowd were wearing "I'm for Jackie" buttons. Most of them were black.

On the field, Jackie seemed comfortable at
first base, helping to turn a double play.
  "Robinson used to play shortstop and
second base," said Matty's father. "But playing
first was his best chance for making the majors."
  When Jackie came up again, Matty held his breath.

This time, Jackie flied out to left field.

"At least he got some wood on it," Matty muttered.

"You stink, Robinson!" someone shouted behind him. "Go back where you belong!"

Matty frowned. He knew how nervous he would be batting in his first major-league game. Maybe Jackie was nervous too. He certainly looked tense his next time up, hitting into a double play.

At the seventh-inning stretch, the Dodgers were behind 3–2.

Matty stood in line to buy a hot dog. Two white kids were talking to a black boy in front of them.

"That's stupid," said one, pointing to the "I'm for Jackie" button the black boy was wearing.

"Negroes should stick to their own kind," said the other. "They'll never make it in the big leagues. Robinson's 0 for 3 today."

"Just you wait," said the black boy. "Jackie will show you. There are plenty of good black players out there."

The first kid laughed. "But this is the majors," he said.

"It sure is," said Matty. "That's why it's so important for the Dodgers to have the best team possible. If some of the best players are black, they're the ones who can help us get to the World Series. That's what we all want, isn't it?"

The boys nodded.

"Everything all right?" asked his father when he got back. "I see you got a button."

Matty nodded. "It was a gift from a new friend."

"Oh?"

"We met these two kids," Matty explained. "They didn't think Jackie belonged on the team."

"And?" his father asked.

Matty grinned. "We straightened them out."

Jackie came to bat again in the bottom of the seventh.

With Eddie Stanky on first, he bunted down the line.

The ball rolled toward first as Jackie ran up the baseline. The first baseman, Earl Torgeson, charged the ball. He fielded it cleanly but hurried his throw.

The ball hit Jackie in the back and rolled into right field.

By the time the right fielder picked it up,
Jackie was on second base. Stanky was on third.
  "Good hustle, Jackie!" yelled Matty.
  His father was impressed. "Did you see that?
He just exploded out of the box!"

The next batter was Pete Reiser.
He was one of Matty's favorites.
"Come on!" said Matty. "We
need to tie it at least."

Reiser hit a double just inside the right-field line. Both runners got home easily. It was Jackie Robinson's first run in the big leagues.

"We're ahead now," said Matty. "Hopefully for keeps."

His hope came true. The Dodgers scored once more that inning and won the game 5–3.

"So what do you think?" Matty's father asked, as they stood to leave.

Matty laughed. "I think the guy you work with is crazy."

"Crazy? Why is that?"

"Because," said Matty, "I wouldn't have missed Jackie Robinson for anything."

As Matty and his father filed out of the stadium, they saw a lot of happy faces.

"I wonder how nervous Jackie was," said Matty. "I'll bet he's glad to have that game behind him."

The Dodgers' new first baseman had done well for a rookie. It was a good sign.

"Watch out, World Series!" Matty shouted. "Here we come!"

This was going to be a season to remember. He just knew it.

The Robinson family poses for a picture. Jackie is second from the left.

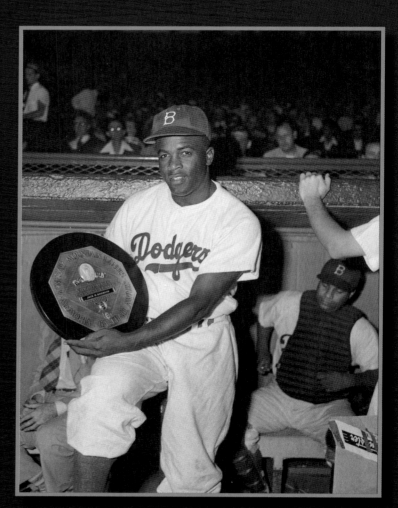

Jackie holds his Most Valuable Player Award.

Jackie plays college football with the University of California at Los Angeles team.

Jackie Robinson was born in Georgia on January 31, 1919. While he was still a baby, his family moved to Pasadena, California. He was the youngest of five children raised by a single mother. Jackie excelled at many sports. At the University of California at Los Angeles (UCLA), he was the first student ever to win letters in four sports—football, basketball, baseball, and track.

In 1945, Jackie played baseball for the Kansas City Monarchs in the Negro Leagues, the only place black men could play professional baseball. (At the time, *Negro* was the word used for black or African American.) Branch Rickey, the president of the Brooklyn Dodgers, was looking for the right player to break baseball's long-established color line, and he picked Robinson. In his autobiography, *I Never Had It Made*, Robinson remembered dealing with "the knowledge that any mistake I made would be magnified because I was the only black man out there."

The Dodgers did win the National League pennant in 1947, though they lost to the New York Yankees in the World Series. All season, Jackie Robinson was treated roughly by many fans and some fellow ballplayers. He hit .297 that year, led the National League with 29 stolen bases, and won the first-ever Rookie of the Year Award. Off the field, he faced racial name-calling, hate letters, and even death threats.

In 1949, Jackie Robinson was the league's Most Valuable Player. He led the Dodgers to a World Series Championship in 1955 and retired the next year. He died at the age of 53 in 1972.

In 1997, on the 50th anniversary of Robinson's first game, he was honored at Shea Stadium in New York, the only remaining National League stadium in the city at the time. During the ceremonies, his number, 42, was retired forever throughout Major League Baseball. On April 15, 2004, baseball commissioner Bud Selig remarked that "baseball's proudest moment and its most powerful social statement came on April 15, 1947, when Jackie Robinson first set foot on a Major League Baseball field."

BOOKS

Editors of Time for Kids. *Time for Kids: Jackie Robinson: Strong Inside and Out.* New York: HarperCollins, 2005. This biography provides a brief overview of Robinson's life, historic photos, and an interview with Robinson's daughter, Sharon.

McPherson, Stephanie Sammartino. *Jackie Robinson.* Minneapolis: Lerner Publications Company, 2010. This biography introduces the life of Jackie Robinson and is illustrated with photos of Robinson, his family, and his friends.

Nelson, Kadir. *We are the Ship: The Story of Negro League Baseball.* New York: Hyperion, 2008. This wonderfully illustrated book tells the history of African Americans and baseball, from the creation of the Negro Leagues to Jackie Robinson playing in Major League Baseball.

Ritter, Lawrence S. *Leagues Apart: The Men and Times of the Negro Baseball Leagues.* New York: Morrow Junior Books, 1999. Read about the history of baseball's Negro Leagues, and find out basic information on some of the league's best players.

Robinson, Sharon. *Testing the Ice: A True Story about Jackie Robinson*. New York: Scholastic Press, 2009.
Jackie Robinson's daughter, Sharon, tells about her father's courage and determination through a story about ice-skating.

WEBSITES

Baseball and Jackie Robinson
http://lcweb2.loc.gov/ammem/collections/robinson/
This Library of Congress site provides a timeline of both Jackie Robinson and baseball, as well as early pictures of baseball games and players.

Negro League Baseball
http://www.negroleaguebaseball.com/
Visit the official site of the Negro Leagues. Read about the different teams, the great players, and the history of the league.

Negro League Baseball Players Association
http://www.nlbpa.com/history.html
Learn about the history of Major League Baseball and the history of the Negro Leagues.

The Official Site of Jackie Robinson
http://www.jackierobinson.com/about/
The official website of Jackie Robinson includes a biography, interviews with Robinson and his family, facts about the baseball legend, and more.

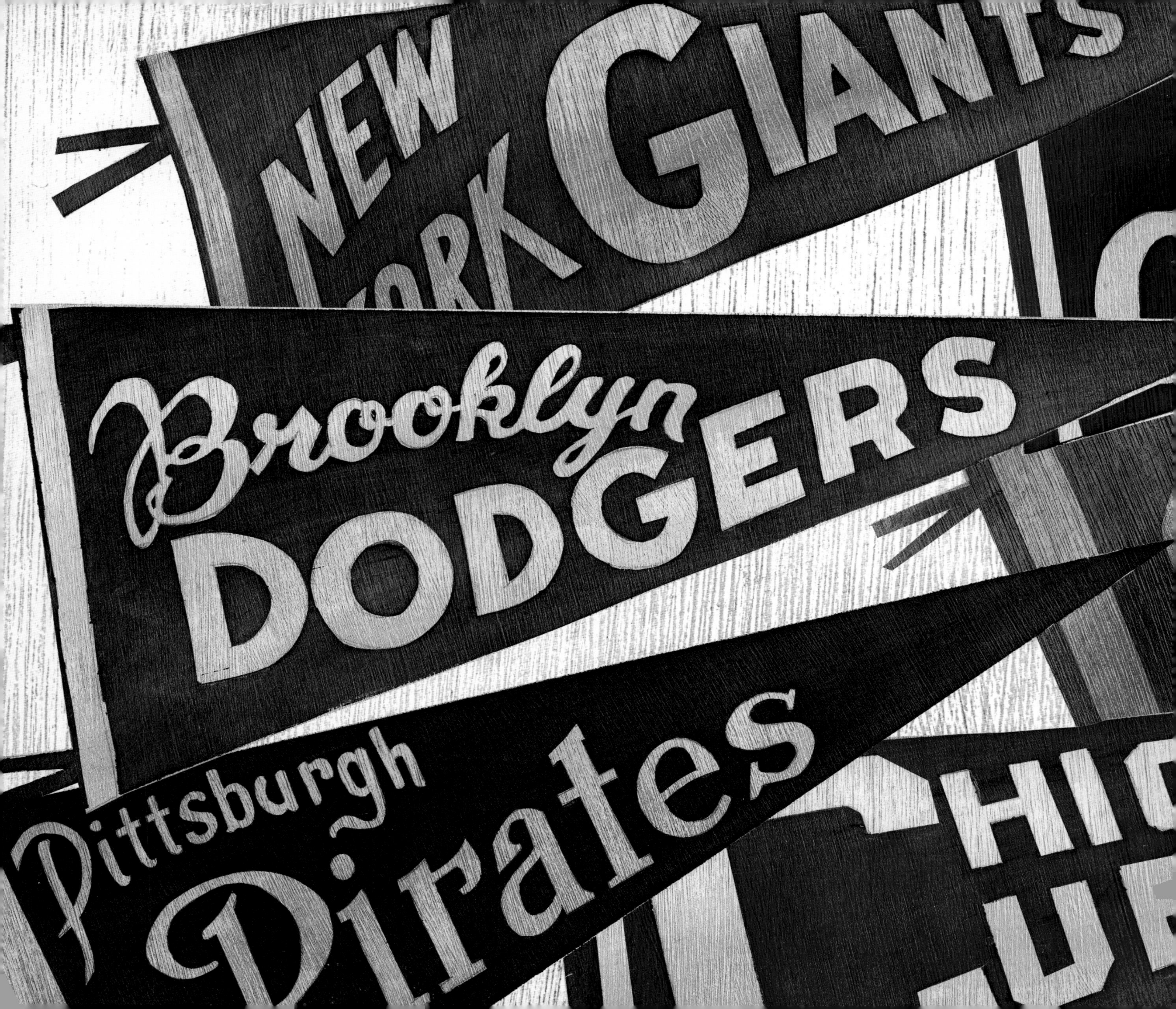
NEW
GIANTS
Brooklyn
DODGERS
Pittsburgh
Pirates